Brave Smiles

...another lesbian tragedy

by The Five Lesbian Brothers
Maureen Angelos, Babs Davy,
Dominique Dibbell,
Peg Healey and Lisa Kron

A SAMUEL FRENCH ACTING EDITION

SAMUEL
FRENCH

FOUNDED 1830

NEW YORK HOLLYWOOD LONDON TORONTO

SAMUELFRENCH.COM

ISBN 978-0-573-69703-6   Printed in U.S.A.   #29099

MUSIC USE NOTE

Licensees are solely responsible for obtaining formal written permission from copyright owners to use copyrighted music in the performance of this play and are strongly cautioned to do so. If no such permission is obtained by the licensee, then the licensee must use only original music that the licensee owns and controls. Licensees are solely responsible and liable for all music clearances and shall indemnify the copyright owners of the play and their licensing agent, Samuel French, Inc., against any costs, expenses, losses and liabilities arising from the use of music by licensees.

IMPORTANT BILLING AND CREDIT REQUIREMENTS

All producers of *BRAVE SMILES... ANOTHER LESBIAN TRAGEDY* must give credit to the Author of the Play in all programs distributed in connection with performances of the Play, and in all instances in which the title of the Play appears for the purposes of advertising, publicizing or otherwise exploiting the Play and/or a production. The name of the Author *must* appear on a separate line on which no other name appears, immediately following the title and *must* appear in size of type not less than fifty percent of the size of the title type.

BRAVE SMILES...ANOTHER LESBIAN TRAGEDY was first produced in January 1992 at the WOW Café in New York City under the direction of Kate Stafford. Sets and costumes were designed by Susan Young, lights were by Joni Wong, sound design was by Peg Healey and the fabulous stage manager was Jimmy Eckerle. The cast was as follows:

MARTHA/THALIA/REPORTER #2.................. Maureen Angelos
MILLICENT / MISS GATEAU / PIERRE.................... Babs Davy
WILL/FRAU LUDMILLA VON PUSSENHEIMER/
    REPORTER #1/AUDREY ....Dominique Dibbell
BABE/MISS GRETA PHILLIPS/
    WOUNDED SOLDIER/SHIRLEY/BUM .... Peg Healey
DAMWELL MAXWELL/BARONESS......................... Lisa Kron
And introducing **NIPPER** as herself

This production was also presented at Downtown Art Company, New York City.

BRAVE SMILES...ANOTHER LESBIAN TRAGEDY was subsequently produced March 1993 in the version printed here at One Dream in New York City with the same cast. The director was Kate Stafford. Set and prop design were by Jamie Leo, costume design was by Susan Young, lights were by Diana Arecco and sound design was by Peg Healey. Musical arrangements were provided by Tom Judson and the Brave Smiles Orchestra.

This production has also been presented at Theatre Rhinoceros, San Francisco; Fresh Dish, San Diego; Highways, Los Angeles; New Prospects, Prospect Park, Brooklyn; DiverseWorks, Houston; Next Stage, Boston; Alice B. Theatre, Seattle; New York Theatre Workshop, New York City; Drill Hall, London and P. S. 122, New York City.

CHARACTERS

MARTHA – deaf-mute, though strangely perceptive.

MILLICENT – sensitive and poetic.

WILL – tomboy butch with bravado.

BABE – athletic with good genes.

DAMWELL MAXWELL – bossy big boots.

THALIA – new girl, Jewess, sad German refugee accent.

MISS GATEAU – French cook, possible alcohol problem.

FRAU LUDMILLA VON PUSSENHEIMER – scary, embittered headmistress, Teutonic accent, forties.

MISS GRETA PHILLIPS – beautiful and bewitching teacher, mid-twenties.

BARONESS – European lower-caste royalty, loaded.

REPORTERS #1 AND #2 – fast-talking newspapermen.

PIERRE – the Parisian maître d'.

AUDREY – Audrey Hepburn-like actress who plays the role of Sharon.

SHIRLEY – Shirley MacLaine-like actress who plays the role of Bertha.

WOUNDED SOLDIER – guy with bad hole in him, the original Vin Marconi.

BUM – man with the D.T.'s.

NIPPER – Babe's canine companion, a hand puppet.

SETTING

ACT I
The Tilue-Pussenheimer Academy, somewhere in Europe, 1920.

Scene One: Mike's Funeral.
Scene Two: Play Practice.
Scene Three: Damwell and Thalia.
Scene Four: Miss Gateau in the Kitchen.
Scene Five: Smoking Club.
Scene Six: Herr Pye.
Scene Seven: Brave Smiles.
Scene Eight: Night Talk.
Scene Nine: Sleeping Girls.
Scene Ten: The Confrontation.
Scene Eleven: Martha Is Dead.
Scene Twelve: Will Leaves.
Scene Thirteen: Frau von Pussenheimer's Farewell.
Scene Fourteen: Miss Phillips's Farewell.

ACT II
Scene One: Damwell's Wedding. The Grand Ballroom of the Hôtel
Goldene Gewölbe, Vienna, 1939.
Scene Two: The Disembarkation. New York Harbor, 1943.
Scene Three: Babe on a Plane.
The cockpit of the Grand Dame, a few weeks later.
Scene Four: Vin's Place. A gay Parisian nightclub, 1946.
Scene Five: The Rehearsal. A Broadway theatre, 1956.
Scene Six: The Mission. The Bowery, 1959.
Scene Seven: I Want to Live. Sing Sing Prison, October 12, 1959.
Scene Eight: The Book Signing. Rizzoli, New York City, 1969.
Scene Nine: Southampton. Later that day.
Scene Ten: Southampton. Two years later.

AUTHORS' NOTES

LISA KRON: I'm trying to remember what the initial seed was for this play. I think we might have had the title left over from a title search for *Voyage to Lesbos* (which, by the way, also included the still unused title, *Lunchtime at the Menstrual Hut or Give Me a Slice of That Fur Pie to Go*). The world has changed so much in the ten years since we started working, long before the regular appearance of lesbian characters in the movies or on TV, certainly long before Ellen DeGeneres. If word went around that some TV show might have a secondary lesbian character skulking around the background, all the gay girls would run home to watch it. There were a handful of iconographic images and they all involved a tragic end for the poor sapphic sufferer.

PEG HEALEY: We watched, read, listened to, explored and absorbed every possible lesbian icon we could get our hands on and shamelessly used them for our own purposes. If the story of the lesbian is that she was always doomed to suffer an unhappy life and then die a tragic death, then we really wanted to pile it on:

Reference Materials

Morocco (Marlene Dietrich)	*The Children's Hour*
Johnny Guitar	*Pentimento*
The Killing of Sister George	*Last Summer at Blue Fish Cove*
Walk on the Wild Side (Jane Fonda and Barbara Stanwyck)	*I Want to Live*
The Well of Loneliness	*Julia*
The Price of Salt	*Maedchen in Uniform*
Ann Bannon's Books	

At this early stage in our relationship our time was divided fifty-fifty between doing the work and working on our relationship. We adopted the strategy of using check-ins to periodically clear the air. They served to remind us that we were all working toward the same thing and kept our meetings from dissolving into the miasma of our own personal hells.

BABS DAVY: We wrote free-writing after free-writing, some as short as a minute, some as long as an hour. We read them aloud and began making lists of images, possible characters and locations. One of us had recently broken up with her longtime girlfriend and much of the deep sadness and sense of loss that comes through in *Brave Smiles* can be traced to that person's poignant writing during this time. In the end we had piles of writing and Dominique volunteered to write the second act and Peg, who was laid up from sinus surgery and couldn't rehearse, volunteered to write the first act.

DOMINIQUE DIBBELL: This was our first play that Kate Stafford directed. She did much to shape our unique performance style with her simple and inventive solutions to the monumental problems we presented her: numerous blackouts, lightning-quick costume changes, a play that wanted to be a movie.

MAUREEN ANGELOS: This play is a reflection of love. They are all labors of love but this one in particular manifests what we love about being Brothers and what we love about being lesbians: the tragedy of it all which can be so bitingly and relentlessly funny sometimes. This play asks the audience why they are laughing and are they sure they're not crying.

*This play is lovingly dedicated to our good friend Jimmy Eckerle,
the bravest smiler.*

ACT I

Scene One
Mike's Funeral

(The grounds of the Tilue-Pussenheimer Academy, once a prestigious school for young ladies, now little more than an orphanage with pretensions. Dawn. Lights fade up slowly. **MILLICENT**, **WILL**, **BABE**, **DAMWELL** *and* **MARTHA** *stand in a semicircle facing the audience, heads bowed.* **MILLICENT** *is at the head of Mike's grave.* **MARTHA** *wears a black veil.)*

MILLICENT. We offer up all our work this day to the memory of Mike, who fought so hard to survive despite the cruel blows of a hatchet wielded by Dick Moorehead, groundskeeper and a misguided heathen –

WILL. And a low-down dog!

MILLICENT. Yes, and unenlightened as to the sanctity of all life and limb...

BABE. Especially the head.

MILLICENT. Yes, which is necessary for mammals if they are to conduct themselves in a spiritual way.

*(***DAMWELL*** starts to leave;* **BABE** *stops her. The girls all gasp and exclaim.)*

DAMWELL. Sorry. I thought she was finished.

WILL. Go on, Millicent.

MILLICENT. So now we commend your soul, Mike, to heaven above or to that watery grave in the well from which you emerged.

BABE. Fear not, Mike, you will be reunited with your beloved head in the great beyond or below...we're not sure which.

WILL. Mike, you gave us many weeks of loyal service as pet of the school, mascot and general chum to all the girls.

MILLICENT. We'll keep you in our prayers. Please keep us in your prayers and put some good words in for us poor little orphan girls here at the Academy. We're not really that bad and we did try to put your head back on. We're sorry about it being separated from your beautiful domed body by Dick, but that's Dick.

(The girls assent.)

Would anyone else care to say a few words?

DAMWELL. Maybe Martha would like to say something.

WILL. Shut up, Damwell!

DAMWELL. What? Everyone knows Martha's a dummy.

(WILL shoves DAMWELL.)

WILL. She's a deaf-mute and brighter than you'll ever be!

(MARTHA runs off. WILL chases her, calling, "Martha! Martha, wait!")

DAMWELL. They make a perfect couple.

MILLICENT. Have you no feelings, Damwell? Really. And at Mike's funeral and all...

DAMWELL. Mike is a turtle! And we're all sixteen and practically adults although no one would guess it from the way you carry on. Come on, Babe.

(BABE doesn't move.)

Babe! *(pause)* I'll see you later at play practice.

(DAMWELL storms off. WILL enters.)

BABE. I – I just think I ought to say something.

WILL. Amen.

BABE. Yes. Amen. And, well, sorry about Damwell.

MILLICENT. Where's Martha?

WILL. In the root cellar. It's OK. She likes it there. That Damwell really galls me.

MILLICENT. Don't let her get to you, Will. Her sense of humor is her armor against cruelty and sadness in this world.

WILL. Yeah, that and the million dollars she inherited ought to give her pretty good protection.

MILLICENT. I believe that money won't be hers until she's twenty-one.

BABE. Damwell's okay. She doesn't mean to hurt anyone.

WILL. She doesn't try to get at you the way she does with me, Babe.

MILLICENT. Maybe Damwell likes you, Will. I mean really likes you.

WILL. *(spitting in the dirt)* Curse the day! Take that spell away!

BABE. She said she liked me.

MILLICENT. I'm sure she does, Babe.

BABE. I'm late for kitchen duty. *(runs off)*

(WILL remains with MILLICENT. There is an awkward silence.)

MILLICENT. It's OK. Go to Martha. I don't mind being alone.

(WILL smiles, kisses MILLICENT gently on the forehead, then runs off.)

Dear God, wherever and whoever you are, please help Martha in all her sadness. Will is trying so hard for her. We all want so much to transform people like they will see and understand that little, hard, green, lesson about life – that you have to accept and love yourself.

(MILLICENT takes out her guitar and sings "Turtles Are Free." [Sheet music for all songs is at the end of the play.] During the song, MISS PHILLIPS enters, smokes a Tiparillo cigar and watches. MILLICENT does not know she's there.)

MILLICENT. *(cont.)*

OH, A TURTLE DIES
AND A YOUNG GIRL CRIES
THE WORLD IS CHANGED FOREVER.

WHEN THE DEATH KNELL RINGS
OH, THE GRIEF! IT BRINGS
BOTH TURTLE AND GIRL TOGETHER.

TUR-TLES ARE FREE
TUR-TLES ARE FREE
TUR-TLES ARE FREE.

OH, A TURTLE'S LIFE
IS A HARD, HARD LIFE –

*(***MISS PHILLIPS*** clears her throat.)*

Oh, Miss Phillips!

MISS PHILLIPS. Don't let me stop you. It's a lovely song.

MILLICENT. It's nothing compared to the poetry you read to us in class.

MISS PHILLIPS. Perhaps one day you will be as great as Sappho. But you must work at it. Here, Millicent –

*(***MISS PHILLIPS*** hands* **MILLICENT** *a doughnut wrapped in a napkin.)*

You missed your breakfast.

MILLICENT. Oh! I must get to breakfast. Frau von Pussenheimer will be –

MISS PHILLIPS. I explained to her that you weren't feeling well.

MILLICENT. But I'm – oh, Miss Phillips...

MISS PHILLIPS. Millicent, I need your help.

MILLICENT. Why...anything.

MISS PHILLIPS. There's a new girl arriving next week. I want you to be kind to her. She'll need a friend. And try to – well, I know you girls have rules about new girls but, Thalia may be in for more difficulty than the rest of us and it is our moral duty to help her.

MILLICENT. Thalia...I'll do what I can.

MISS PHILLIPS. Good. Eat your breakfast. And don't be late for your French lesson.

(She exits, giving **MILLICENT***'s rear a gentle pinch.)*

MILLICENT. *(opening the napkin)* Oh, Miss Phillips! A sugar doughnut!

(blackout)

Scene Two
Play Practice

(BABE duels with FRAU VON PUSSENHEIMER while DAMWELL and MILLICENT look on. PUSSENHEIMER attacks ferociously until she has backed BABE into a corner and then flings the foil from BABE's hand, cutting her. BABE cries out.)

FRAU VON PUSSENHEIMER. Nonsense. It's a slight flesh wound. I'm very disappointed in you, Babe. Romeo is supposed to win the fight.

DAMWELL. Yeah, Babe.

MILLICENT. Frau von Pussenheimer, couldn't we just *act* like she wins the fight?

(FRAU VON PUSSENHEIMER wheels around to face MILLICENT, whipping her foil through the air.)

FRAU VON PUSSENHEIMER. Good stage fighting is essential to good theatre!

DAMWELL. Shouldn't we practice the scene where I'm a snowy dove showing over crows? After all, isn't Will supposed to be in the fighting scene?

(The girls gasp in unison at DAMWELL's faux pas.)

FRAU VON PUSSENHEIMER. Where is Wilhelmina?

(The girls all sputter different explanations.)

Never mind. She'll be dealt with later. Millicent – bring the gear to the equipment shed and return at once. No dillydallying under the trees.

(She goes to DAMWELL and gets uncomfortably close.)

Now, Damwell. You wish to be a snowy dove trooping with crows, do you? Tell me, have you ever attempted a stage kiss?

DAMWELL. Actually...Babe and I have been practicing... every night...I think we...

FRAU VON PUSSENHEIMER. Don't be silly. You and Babe are merely girls. You have no idea how a man might kiss a woman. Whereas I, although I remain an honest woman, have had some experience which might benefit you.

*(*DAMWELL *and* BABE *look ill at the prospect of kissing* FRAU VON PUSSENHEIMER.*)*

DAMWELL. Oh but...I doubt that Romeo kisses anything like Professor Pye.

*(*BABE *and* DAMWELL *gasp.)*

Oh, Frau von Pussenheimer, I'm so sorry...

FRAU VON PUSSENHEIMER. *(smiling a crazy smile)* It's quite all right girls. I suppose it's only natural you should talk of such things amongst yourselves. I have taken no offense. Although you'd be surprised at the professor's passion. Why, I must confess, it takes everything I have to resist Herr...Peter.

DAMWELL. His first name's Peter? What does he look –

FRAU VON PUSSENHEIMER. *(becoming quite unfriendly)* That's enough of that. Soon you will know all of my secrets and we can't have that, can we?

MILLICENT. *(from offstage)* Frau von Pussenheimer! Babe! Come quick. It's Thalia! The new girl!!

*(*BABE *starts to run off.* FRAU VON PUSSENHEIMER *indicates that* BABE *is to walk, not run. Then she nods to* DAMWELL *to go as well.* BABE *and* DAMWELL *meet* MILLICENT *as she enters with* THALIA, *who is disheveled.)*

I found her out by the river, near the shed.

FRAU VON PUSSENHEIMER. Well, her coat is certainly a mess.

THALIA. It's not my fault. I was attacked!

DAMWELL. *(thinking it's the coolest thing ever)* Attacked?!

THALIA. Yes. I arrived in Schlongbahd on the 12:35 train from Vienna. I'm supposed to look for a Ludmilla von Pussenheimer at the Tilue-Pussenheimer Academy.

FRAU VON PUSSENHEIMER. Well, you've found us.

(**FRAU VON PUSSENHEIMER** *approaches* **THALIA.** *The other girls instinctively step back.*)

But we weren't expecting you until next week.

THALIA. My mother wanted me to leave sooner than planned –

BABE & MILLICENT. You have a mother!?

DAMWELL. You were attacked!?

THALIA. When no one met me at the train I set off to find you on my own. Just past the crossroads by the tall hedges – a band of wild boys jumped out at me.

DAMWELL. You were beaten up by a band of wild boys?!

THALIA. They didn't beat me – exactly.

FRAU VON PUSSENHEIMER. What did happen? Exactly.

THALIA. Their leader-boy said, "We just want to talk to you. You have such pretty black hair." They stood around me. They all laughed. That awful boy walked right up to me and said, "Are you afraid of boys?" "No," I said. "You're not afraid of us?" he asked again. "Why should I be? You're just boys."

MILLICENT. How brave...

THALIA. And then...then...

FRAU VON PUSSENHEIMER. What happened?

THALIA. Then he said, "Then you wouldn't mind if we tried to kiss you?" "Well," I said. I knew I shouldn't. But I didn't want them thinking I was afraid of them. "Then you'd let me kiss you?" And he did. But softly. Not like you would expect from such a rough boy. I began to cry. Then they pushed me into the mud and rubbed it in my hair. They turned my coat inside out. Oh, they weren't boys at all. They were beasts! They were horrible, horrible beasts.

FRAU VON PUSSENHEIMER. Filthy boys! No better than pigs!! Remember that, girls. Boys are pigs. Filthy and disgusting!

DAMWELL, BABE & MILLICENT. *(reciting their lesson)* Filthy and disgusting!

FRAU VON PUSSENHEIMER. *(trying to soothe* **THALIA***)* There, there, girl. Damwell, bring Thalia to the dormer in the east wing. Babe, fetch Miss Gateau to tend to her there.

*(**DAMWELL**, **THALIA** *and* **BABE** *exit.)*

Millicent, remain with me a moment.

MILLICENT. Yes, Frau von Pussenheimer?

FRAU VON PUSSENHEIMER. Chocolate, Millicent?

(Tempts her with a giant chocolate bar. **MILLICENT** *takes it.)*

How did you know that Thalia was to be a new student here?

MILLICENT. I don't know, Frau von Pussenheimer. I guess... I guess she must have told me so.

FRAU VON PUSSENHEIMER. I see. You found her face down in a puddle and she told you her name was Thalia and she was to be a new student here?

MILLICENT. Yes. I'm sure now that she told me.

FRAU VON PUSSENHEIMER. Very well.

(awkward pause)

MILLICENT. Am I excused?

FRAU VON PUSSENHEIMER. Well now, Millicent, that is between you and your god, isn't it?

MILLICENT. Pardon?

FRAU VON PUSSENHEIMER. You see, Millicent, little girls who lie seldom become saints and they invariably end up burning in eternal hell. You may go.

*(**MILLICENT** *scurries out. Cross-fade.)*

Scene Three
Damwell and Thalia

(The main hall. **DAMWELL** *is taking* **THALIA** *to her room.)*

DAMWELL. Well, there's a girl who moos at night. But hopefully you won't be put next to her.

THALIA. Such grand halls. Just like Mother said. But why are they so dark?

DAMWELL. Things aren't what they used to be. But you'll find that out soon enough. I'm sure if my mother had known what a hellhole this would turn into she never would have sent me here but...well...did you hear about the *Lusitania?*

Scene Four
Miss Gateau in the Kitchen

*(The kitchen. **MISS GATEAU** is cooking and sipping from a bottle of champagne. **FRAU VON PUSSENHEIMER** sneaks up behind her and whacks her on the butt with a wooden spoon.)*

FRAU VON PUSSENHEIMER *(playfully)* I'm very mad at you, Miss Gateau. You made a soufflé and it fell. Bad, bad girl. *(goes to whack her again)*

MISS GATEAU. Forget it, Ludmilla. I'm not in the mood.

FRAU VON PUSSENHEIMER. *(not so playful anymore)* What are you hiding from me? Sometimes I wonder if you are to be trusted –

MISS GATEAU. Me? Whatever – don't be silly!

FRAU VON PUSSENHEIMER. I am never silly, Colette. You would do well to remember that. You will come to see me in my room later tonight?

MISS GATEAU. Not tonight. I am busy.

FRAU VON PUSSENHEIMER. You are...teaching one of the students a French lesson?

MISS GATEAU. No.

FRAU VON PUSSENHEIMER. Then you are, perhaps, washing your hair?

MISS GATEAU. No.

FRAU VON PUSSENHEIMER. You're going to see Dick.

MISS GATEAU. Yes. Yes, I am. What of it?

FRAU VON PUSSENHEIMER. Tell me, this Dick – he is a tender lover to you?

MISS GATEAU. He is my beau!

FRAU VON PUSSENHEIMER. I am your beau! I am your beau! And your doctor! And your mother! And your father!

MISS GATEAU. I am someone else's daughter, Ludmilla. I have a mother already. See?

*(She shows **FRAU VON PUSSENHEIMER** her locket.)*

MISS GATEAU. *(cont.)* You cannot possess me like you possess the girls. I am a woman. I am not so naive and fresh for the picking as a herd of fifteen year olds! If I wish to have a beau, I will have a beau. Besides, it is for the best.

(**BABE** *enters. They don't see her.*)

FRAU VON PUSSENHEIMER. That thing. That killer of turtles! He is not your lover. Your diversion. Your barbe, perhaps. But not your lover.

(**FRAU VON PUSSENHEIMER** *kisses* **MISS GATEAU** *deeply.*)

Now. I have lubricated you for your date.

(**MISS GATEAU** *slaps* **FRAU VON PUSSENHEIMER**. **FRAU VON PUSSENHEIMER** *notices* **BABE** *in the doorway.*)

How long have you been standing there, dumb ox?

MISS GATEAU. Babe is on kitchen duty, Frau von Pussenheimer.

FRAU VON PUSSENHEIMER *(grabbing her by the ear and pulling her into the room)* Don't let her near the knives, Miss Gateau, the girl is clumsy with a blade. We don't want her cutting her precious hands off. And wash these hands before you touch anything. They're filthy. Carry on, Miss Gateau. *(She exits.)*

BABE. I wish I weren't so clumsy.

MISS GATEAU. Yes, well. Wishes are funny. I used to wish I were my Aunt Elizabeth who used to get into the broom closet and grunt.

BABE. Really?

MISS GATEAU. Oh my, yes. She used to tell me, "Beware of Tiparillo-smoking women. They will always surprise you."

BABE. What did she mean by that?

MISS GATEAU. Ha! She said, "Never trust a man in a hat."

BABE. But that's ridiculous; all men wear hats!

MISS GATEAU. *Exactement! (swallows a glass of champagne, then pours another)* Let me tell you a little something about us French. Once we open a bottle of champagne, we must drink it all at once *parce que* it is all downhill from there. *(She swallows another glass.) Vive la France!* Get the beans.

BABE. I wish I could speak French like you.

MISS GATEAU. Oh, *merde.*

BABE. Maird!

MISS GATEAU. No, no, no. *(drawing it out) Merde.*

BABE. Mairrrrd.

MISS GATEAU. No, no, no. Here, try this. Take a sip of this.

BABE. But that's champagne.

MISS GATEAU. *Oui.* It will help you to speak the French. Take a small sip.

(**BABE** *takes a sip.*)

Don't swallow! Now, say *merde.*

BABE. *(gargling)* Merrrrde.

MISS GATEAU. *Très bien!*

(They kiss Continental style. Blackout.)

Scene Five
Smoking Club

(The basement where the girls have their secret club. **BABE** *and* **WILL** *play cards.* **DAMWELL** *sneaks up on them.)*

DAMWELL. *(imitating Frau von Pussenheimer)* Come, come! Where are your brave smiles?! Remember girls, smile unt za vurld smiles bock!

*(***WILL*** *and* ***BABE*** *ignore* ***DAMWELL.****)*

What are we waiting for?

BABE & WILL. Millicent.

DAMWELL. Oh hell, she doesn't even inhale. Come on, pass out the goods.

*(***WILL*** *lights a Tiparillo, and they pass it around.)*

What a day it's been. We've got so much to talk about.

BABE. I know! I heard Frau von Pussenheimer talking with Miss Gateau about Professor Pye –

DAMWELL. Oh that! That's old news. His first name's Peter, by the way, which information I got straight from the horseface's mouth just as she was about to try to plant one on me.

BABE. I know. I was there.

DAMWELL. But I'm talking about the new girl. Will, you missed rehearsal, for which I'm sure you'll get skinned alive by the way, even though I tried to cover for you, so you haven't seen her yet. But she was attacked by – Hey, don't you even want to hear about her?

BABE. Will and I had to get Martha out of the root cellar again.

DAMWELL. Oh. Sorry.

WILL. Shut up, Damwell.

DAMWELL. Really I am. I don't think she's ever been this bad.

MILLICENT. *(offstage)* Code of honor, sisters in sin! Open the doors and let us in!

DAMWELL. You can cut the secret-club crap, Millicent. I think we're a little old for that.

(**MILLICENT** *enters with* **THALIA.**)

MILLICENT. Hi! Sorry we're late.

DAMWELL. What do you mean "we"? What's she doing here?

MILLICENT. Thalia, this is Damwell.

THALIA. I know Damwell. You brought me to my room.

MILLICENT. And this is Babe.

THALIA. You fetched Miss Gateau for me.

MILLICENT. And this is Will.

THALIA. *(a little stunned)* Oh...Oh...

WILL. She's not supposed to be here. No offense, but this is a secret club. Members only.

MILLICENT. Want a Tiparillo?

(**WILL** *grabs the Tiparillo back from* **MILLICENT.**)

DAMWELL. Will's right. Members only. No offense, Thalia. But you would have to be initiated first.

THALIA. *(leaving)* Sure. I understand.

DAMWELL. *(grabbing* **THALIA**) Wait! You want to join us, don't you?

MILLICENT. Of course she does. All you have to do is take the secret oath. It's nothing. Just repeat after me –

DAMWELL. This special circumstance calls for special measures. Since Thalia has already seen our secret place, and she already knows we smoke, the oath alone isn't enough. She must pass the test.

MILLICENT. What test?

DAMWELL. The TEST. The test of spirit, brains and loyalty. Everyone come here. Thalia, stay there.

WILL. This is stupid, Damwell. You said yourself we're too old for this.

DAMWELL. Will? What's wrong with you? You're always first in line for a little fun.

BABE. Maybe Will's right, Damwell. Why don't we just let her join the club?

DAMWELL. We're not gonna hurt her, we're just gonna have a little fun, that's all. It's not like we get a new girl our age every day.

MILLICENT. We can't do anything to hurt her. I promised.

DAMWELL. Oh, some secret club! Why don't we just invite all the fourteen year-olds over for a smoke. Now. I've got an idea. Babe, get the old wool blanket. We're going to do the desert survival test.

BABE, WILL & MILLICENT. *(horrified)* Oooohhh!

DAMWELL. Come on. It's a fair test, and no one gets hurt.

MILLICENT. OK...

(*They all go over to* **THALIA**, *surrounding her.*)

OK. It's agreed. If you pass a simple survival test, you can be in our club.

THALIA. Well...

DAMWELL. Otherwise we can't let you out alive.

BABE & MILLICENT. Damwell!

DAMWELL. It's a joke!

WILL. She's just kidding. It is a simple test, really.

THALIA. OK then.

DAMWELL. All right. This is a test to see how strong you are mentally and spiritually. Because once you take the oath, we have to be able to rely on you to keep the law of silence about the club – even if von Pussenheimer herself tortures you. Now sit over there.

(**THALIA** *sits on a crate.*)

MILLICENT. Don't be afraid.

THALIA. I'm not afraid.

DAMWELL. Good. Now, we're gonna put this blanket over you.

(**DAMWELL** *covers* **THALIA** *with the blanket.*)

DAMWELL. *(cont.)* And so it begins. Imagine, Thalia, that you're in the desert. It's one hundred and fifty degrees in the shade – if there was any shade, which there's not. You're burning up with heat. You're parched *(She fake coughs.)* with thirst. There's only one thing you can do in this situation to make yourself feel better and that's if you take something off. What are you going to take off, Thalia?

THALIA. What?

DAMWELL. You're hot. It's a million degrees out. You're boiling up. Take something off!

(There's movement underneath the blanket.)

Did you take something off?

THALIA. Yes.

DAMWELL. Well, what is it?

*(**THALIA** pushes her shoes out from under the blanket.)*

Good, Thalia. Now, it's hours later and even hotter than before. Don't you think you should take something else off?

*(**THALIA**'s socks come out from under the blanket.)*

You're being a bit conservative here, Thalia. Because now, now it's high noon and the sun is beating down on you...Beating down on you so hard that blisters are starting to form all over your body...pus-ey, bloody blisters. And as the wind blows, the blisters break and sand mixes with the pus and the blood. Don't you think you should take something else off? What would really cool you down?

*(**THALIA**'s frock comes out.)*

Good, Thalia. That feels better. Now you're walking over hills of sand, miles and miles of sand as far as the eye can see...Oh! Look, Thalia! In the distance, a little pond and some palm trees. Run for it, Thalia! Run for it! You're almost there, you can taste the water...Oh, no! It's a mirage! What a cruel circumstance! You'd better take something else off.

(THALIA's underpants come out. **BABE** *picks them up.* **DAMWELL** *grabs them and takes a sniff.)*

DAMWELL. *(cont.)* Good, Thalia, good.

*(***BABE***, hurt and alarmed, grabs them back.* **MILLICENT** *tries to comfort her.)*

What can you take off now?

THALIA. Nothing.

DAMWELL. Nothing?

MILLICENT. Think, Thalia! Think!

DAMWELL. *(grabbing* **MILLICENT** *to make her be quiet)* That's right, Thalia, think. Surely there's something else you can take off.

THALIA. No, there's nothing. Nothing's left.

DAMWELL. Oh, but there is, Thalia! Why are you in the middle of the boiling hot desert wearing a *wool blanket over your head?*

*(***DAMWELL*** *rips off the blanket to expose* **THALIA.** **WILL** *rushes toward* **THALIA** *and covers her with the blanket.)*

Will! We're supposed to see her naked!

WILL. That's enough, Damwell. It's not funny.

THALIA. You're all sick. All of you! *(to* **WILL***)* And you're the worst! How can you even pretend to be kind after you tricked me and threw me down in the mud? I should have known the minute I saw you here there would be trouble.

MILLICENT. Will, that was you?

WILL. We didn't know it was her. We thought she was some rich girl from town.

THALIA. So that makes it all right to torture people?

BABE & MILLICENT. Will!

WILL. We were just having some fun! We were playing field hockey and –

THALIA. And you decided to terrorize me! Torturing a person for no other reason than she is a Jew.

DAMWELL. A Jew?

MILLICENT. *(simultaneously)* Thalia! Gosh! We didn't know you were a Jew.

WILL. *(simultaneously)* Geez, I'm sorry, Thalia.

BABE. *(simultaneously)* I never saw a Jew before.

MILLICENT. When I joined the club, they made me wear my underwear outside my stockings for a whole week. I remember now how terrified I was, but looking back it seemed all in good fun. Please forgive us, Thalia.

DAMWELL. Are you really a Jew?

THALIA. Yes, I am. And proud of it, too.

DAMWELL. Well, then.

> *(tense pause)*

You're my first Jewish friend, ever.

THALIA. So? Have I passed your initiation?

WILL. *(takes out her penknife)* Come on everyone.

> *(They all gather in a circle around* **WILL.** *Each girl gasps when* **WILL** *cuts their thumbs;* **THALIA** *remains impassive.* **WILL** *cuts her own thumb, suppressing a cry. They press their thumbs together, mingling their blood.)*

WILL. I swear by this blood oath...

MILLICENT, BABE, DAMWELL & THALIA. I swear by this blood oath...

WILL. To always and forever...

MILLICENT, BABE, DAMWELL & THALIA. To always and forever...

WILL. Until each and everyone of us is completely dead...

MILLICENT, BABE, DAMWELL & THALIA. Until each and everyone of us is completely dead...

WILL. Be a true and honorable blood sister...

MILLICENT, BABE, DAMWELL & THALIA. Be a true and honorable blood sister...

WILL. and never to part...

MILLICENT, BABE, DAMWELL & THALIA. and never to part...

ALL. So say we one, so say we all.

(Each girl kisses her own thumb, then puts it to the lips of the girl on her right. They sing "The T-Puss Fight Song":)

MILLICENT, WILL, BABE & DAMWELL.

OHHHH...WHO'S THE BRAVEST SMILER
AT TILUE-PUSSENHEIMER
IT'S THALIA, IT'S THALIA, IT'S THAL...

SHE'S A GREAT BIG DOLL...
BUT WE LOVE HER ANYWAY...

(cross-fade)

Scene Six
Herr Pye

(The grounds of the Academy. Afternoon. **MILLICENT** *flagellates herself with a switch.* **MISS PHILLIPS** *interrupts her.)*

MISS PHILLIPS. Millicent!

MILLICENT. Yes, Miss Phillips.

MISS PHILLIPS. What are you doing?

MILLICENT. My heart is wicked and full of impure thoughts.

MISS PHILLIPS. What thoughts, Millicent?

MILLICENT. Bad, nasty things. Things about Frau von Pussenheimer.

MISS PHILLIPS. Frau von Pussenheimer?

MILLICENT. Yes. She and Professor Pye.

MISS PHILLIPS. *Professor* Pye?

MILLICENT. Professor Peter Pye.

MISS PHILLIPS. Peter Pye is no professor, I assure you.

MILLICENT. Oh. Not a professor? But then how would one address him?

MISS PHILLIPS. As you would address any man of German extraction, I suppose. Herr Peter, or, if you like, Herr Pye. Millicent, why such concern with Frau von Pussenheimer's friend?

MILLICENT. I don't know, Miss Phillips. Frau von Pussenheimer talks about him, little comments here and there about she and her Herr Pye. And they roll over and over in my mind. What if I had a Herr Pye? What horrible things would I do? *(She begins to beat herself again.)* Filthy! Dirty!

MISS PHILLIPS. Millicent, please stop.

MILLICENT. *(throwing her arms around* **MISS PHILLIPS***)* Oh, Miss Phillips! You're my favorite teacher. Is that wretched of me?

MISS PHILLIPS. Caring for someone is never wretched. It often feels wretched, of course, but intellectually we must remember that loving is good.

MILLICENT. Oh, Miss Phillips. What an exquisite thing to say. I must write it in my diary.

MISS PHILLIPS. I have a better idea. Here. *(removing a necklace from around her neck)*

MILLICENT. Your necklace! Oh no. It's so beautiful and I am so plain, so poor and so orphaned, and so full of nasty, nasty thoughts.

MISS PHILLIPS. You remind me of myself when I was a girl. This necklace was a gift from a teacher of mine, as a matter of fact. Her name was Frau von Pussenheimer. Seventeen years ago she and I had a talk right here in this very garden when she discovered me wearing a hair shirt. It is a necklace of tears, Millicent. Another bead is added every time crushing disappointment comes your way. When Frau von Pussenheimer gave it to me, it held but a single bead. And now...well, my beloved teacher is a raving lunatic with a drinking problem and the necklace is yours. Perhaps some day you will pass it on as well, my beautiful student with the nasty, nasty thoughts.

*(**MISS PHILLIPS** kisses **MILLICENT** on the forehead. Lights fade out.)*

Scene Seven
Brave Smiles

(The main hall. **MILLICENT**, **DAMWELL** *and* **THALIA**
sing a choral arrangement, "Brave Smiles," with **FRAU**
VON PUSSENHEIMER *conducting.)*

MILLICENT, DAMWELL & THALIA.
BRAVE SMILES
TRY TO HOLD YOUR CHIN HIGH
BRAVE SMILES
SHOULDERS STRAIGHT AND DON'T CRY
LIFE IS HARD
IT MAY BE SO
IT ALL DEPENDS ON YOU
A BRAVE SMILE
CAN HELP TO PULL YOU THROUGH.

FRAU VON PUSSENHEIMER. Beautiful...that was very beautiful, girls. *(gazing at a portrait of Frau Tilue on horseback,*
which hangs on the wall) Frau Tilue would have been
very proud of you. Frau Tilue loves you girls. You are
her sponges. Her sad, beautiful little sponges soaking
up the knowledge. Now, I want to see clean hands for
dinner! Understood? *(She exits.)*

DAMWELL. What did I tell you? "Brave Smiles" again. This is
real trouble. She's even been hitting the sauce.

THALIA. She didn't seem drunk to me.

DAMWELL. Any time she starts talking about Tilue it's a sure
bet. The question is: how far into the label is she?

THALIA. What do you mean?

MILLICENT. She means she wonders how much liquor Frau
von Pussenheimer has taken.

*(***BABE*** rushes in, breathless.)*

DAMWELL. Babe! Where's Will?

BABE. Shhh. I'll explain later.

DAMWELL. Great. Now it's curtains for all of us.

FRAU VON PUSSENHEIMER. *(entering)* Line up. Present hands.

> *(The girls present their hands.* **FRAU VON PUSSENHEIMER** *moves along the line, inspecting them.)*

Good, Millicent. Very good, Thalia...Damwell. Babe! Your nails are a filthy mess. I want them scrubbed, do you hear me? Scrub them until they are raw and maybe then you may return to the supper table.

BABE. Yes, ma'am. *(scurries off)*

FRAU VON PUSSENHEIMER. How you girls expect to be fed when all day long you are digging in the dirt like little doggies is a mystery to me. Anyway, tonight for after dinner Miss Gateau has prepared a special treat in honor of the new girl. Tell me, Thalia, do you like *hamantaschen?*

THALIA. A *hamantaschen?* For me?

FRAU VON PUSSENHEIMER. Yes, that's right.

> *(***FRAU VON PUSSENHEIMER*** *hands out bowls and spoons.* **BABE** *enters.)*

I hope you girls appreciate our Miss Gateau. She is a woman of extraordinary talents. *(smiling to herself)* Hmmmm. *(inspecting* **BABE***'s hands)* Much better, Babe. Now. You may begin eating. And remember: I want no slurping.

> *(***DAMWELL*** *slurps her soup.* **FRAU VON PUSSENHEIMER** *turns and, thinking it's nothing, turns away.* **DAMWELL** *slurps again.* **FRAU VON PUSSENHEIMER** *catches her.)*

BABE. Damwell, quit it.

DAMWELL. What?! I can't help it.

FRAU VON PUSSENHEIMER. Is the soup to your taste, Damwell?

DAMWELL. Lovely, Frau von Pussenheimer.

FRAU VON PUSSENHEIMER. Perhaps it's too much to ask you to enjoy your meal in silence?

DAMWELL. No, ma'am. *(She is smiling. It's a nervous reaction that she cannot control.)*

FRAU VON PUSSENHEIMER. Perhaps you would like to share your amusement with the rest of us.

DAMWELL. Pardon?

FRAU VON PUSSENHEIMER. What is it that you find so funny?

DAMWELL. Nothing.

(All the girls snicker and try to suppress their laughter.)

FRAU VON PUSSENHEIMER. Babe?

BABE. Yes, ma'am.

FRAU VON PUSSENHEIMER. Where is Wilhelmina?

BABE. Who?

FRAU VON PUSSENHEIMER. That's not funny. Where is she? What's going on?

DAMWELL. I – I think she was helping Dick Moorehead mend the fence. I think that's what she said. He needed help and Will was the only one strong enough –

FRAU VON PUSSENHEIMER. Liar! Will is not with Dick Moorehead! Where is she? Speak one or you will all suffer! Millicent?

MILLICENT. I don't know, ma'am. I haven't seen Will since before –

FRAU VON PUSSENHEIMER. Ha! I already know you're a liar. Babe?

BABE. I haven't seen her since –

FRAU VON PUSSENHEIMER. Liars! Liars! All of you! Hiding something from me. Conspiring behind Frau von Pussenheimer's back. Perhaps you are trying to play a practical joke on Frau von Pussenheimer. Is that it? Perhaps you have pinned a humorous message to the back of my frock! *(twists around, trying to see her own back)* After all I've done for you. This is how you show your gratefulness? Well, I won't have it! Go to your rooms! Go!

*(The girls rush out. **FRAU VON PUSSENHEIMER** is left alone with the portrait of Frau Tilue. She talks to it.)*

FRAU VON PUSSENHEIMER. *(cont.)* Oh, Emmeline. Why have you leaved me? They used to love me, the girls. They used to vie for my attention. Why, just a look from me would be all a girl could ever hope for or dream of. Now they are lost to me. Someone is stealing them away. Yes. Someone is usurping me. Trouble has come to live at the Academy...and I know just how to root it out.

(blackout)

Scene Eight
Night Talk

(The bedroom. Nighttime. From offstage, a girl moos.)

DAMWELL. There goes that horrible mooing girl.

(The girl moos again.)

Girl! I'll give you twenty cents if you stop that mooing.

(another moo)

Babe.

BABE. What, Damwell?

DAMWELL. I can't sleep. That girl is mooing again. I need you to rub on me or I'll never sleep.

BABE. I can't.

DAMWELL. I'll give you three dollars if you come rub on me.

BABE. I'm all bloody again. It already happened. I don't know why I'm bloody again.

DAMWELL. You dunce! It happens every month.

BABE. Every month! You didn't tell me that. What about the match tomorrow?

DAMWELL. Well, you can't play. And I don't think you should wash either.

MILLICENT. She has to do something. If her sheets are bloody, she'll catch it from Frau von Pussenheimer.

BABE. What will I do?

WILL. Hold it in.

DAMWELL. You'll have to sleep in the washroom.

BABE. But I'll be so cold.

DAMWELL. Do you want to catch it from Frau von Pussenheimer?

*(**BABE** exits. **THALIA** is crying.)*

Shhh! New girl! Shhh!

WILL. Leave her alone, Damwell. She's an orphan.

DAMWELL. I've got news for you. We're all orphans. Besides, I heard she's got parents.

MILLICENT. I have two parents.

(**DAMWELL** *and* **WILL** *groan.*)

I do so. I have a mother and a dad and we live on Strawberry Lane in the village of Hootsville. When I grow up, I'm going to run an orphanage made of toast. Warm, buttery toast. So at night, when you feel like crying, you can take a nibble.

DAMWELL. Silly. If you took a bite of toast every time you were hungry or sad you'd weigh in at twelve stone.

(**THALIA** *continues to cry.*)

Girl, stop that crying. I'll give you twenty cents if you stop that crying. Be sensible. All your people are sensible. That's what our maid used to say. That's why your people have pots of money.

WILL. Damwell, you're an oaf. You're the rich one.

DAMWELL. Oh! You're right. (*She laughs and laughs.*)

MILLICENT. Damwell! Can't you be quieter? What if Pussenheimer hears you?

DAMWELL. What if she does? Why, if she came in here right now, I'd say, "I'm so sorry to bother you, Ludmilla. But Wilhelmina was just telling us of how often she dreams of kissing you."

WILL. Damn you, Damwell!

(**WILL** *jumps on* **DAMWELL**. *They start wrestling around.*)

MILLICENT. Stop it, you two! What if Pussenheimer hears you and comes in instead of Miss Phillips!

(*They quiet down immediately.*)

THALIA. Who is Miss Phillips?

DAMWELL. You haven't met Miss Phillips?

MILLICENT. (*simultaneously*) She's is our guardian angel.

WILL. (*simultaneously*) She's beautiful.

DAMWELL. *(simultaneously)* She's heavenly. When she looks at you directly in your eyes, you could just faint and die from it.

*(**MILLICENT** and **WILL** assent.)*

MILLICENT. You'll see.

WILL. She comes to tuck us in each night.

DAMWELL. And sometimes, when the mood strikes her, she gives us each a little kiss.

(All three girls sigh. There is a pause.)

MILLICENT. Will, tell us a story.

WILL. One night, I slipped away from the school. A truck drove by and I hopped on the back. I dozed. I dreamt of the ocean and a night full of stars. An old sailor man found me. He said, "Hey, boy, come here." He felt in my pants. He didn't find what he was looking for and said, "Damn." He shoved me. I fell out of the back and ran. Later I became a star in Paris.

THALIA. That's not true!

WILL. It is!

MILLICENT. She's coming.

(All the girls scurry into their proper beds.)

MISS PHILLIPS. Good evening, girls.

GIRLS. Good evening, Miss Phillips.

MISS PHILLIPS. *(kissing each girl on the forehead as she goes)* Good night, Damwell. Will, sleep tight. Millicent, don't let the bedbugs bite. Little Thalia. Welcome to the Academy.

*(**MISS PHILLIPS** kisses **THALIA** sweetly on the lips. Tantalized, she comes in for another, this one turns into an exaggerated, deep, tonsil-licking kiss.)*

I'll see you in the morning, girls.

*(**MISS PHILLIPS** exits. **DAMWELL**, **MILLICENT** and **WILL** swoon. **THALIA** is mystified but not complaining.)*

(fade to black)

Scene Nine
Sleeping Girls

(Silent scene: **DAMWELL**, **MILLICENT** *and* **THALIA** *all feel each other up in their sleep.)*

(fade to black)

Scene Ten
The Confrontation

(FRAU VON PUSSENHEIMER's office.)

MISS PHILLIPS. It's awfully late. Is this business?

FRAU VON PUSSENHEIMER. What else would it be? It's my sad duty to tell you, Miss Phillips, that you are dismissed.

MISS PHILLIPS. Dismissed? But why?

FRAU VON PUSSENHEIMER. You disagree with the Tilue-Pussenheimer method. You're subverting me in the classroom and on the athletic fields.

MISS PHILLIPS. Frau von Pussenheimer, girls must have a little kind attention once in a while.

FRAU VON PUSSENHEIMER. It's a dangerous world. A world made for men and not women. We can't allow the girls to leave here with their hearts so wide open and trusting. They'll be walking targets.

MISS PHILLIPS. But you're so hard on them.

FRAU VON PUSSENHEIMER. How do you propose to maintain order?

MISS PHILLIPS. With love.

FRAU VON PUSSENHEIMER. That's manipulative. Miss Phillips, you've been out in the world. I don't have to tell you what kind of options there are out there for girls.

MISS PHILLIPS. But there are, Frau von Pussenheimer. There are places – nightclubs, writing circles –

FRAU VON PUSSENHEIMER. You are idealistic. And yet here you are. Back in the wet, echoey halls of Tilue-Pussenheimer Academy.

MISS PHILLIPS. Yes.

FRAU VON PUSSENHEIMER. As I recall, you were all too eager to leave the Academy when you turned seventeen. As I recall, you wouldn't accept the gift I tried to give you.

MISS PHILLIPS. I didn't want your stupid hairbrush! I didn't want anything from you. You used me. You played me like the grand piano in the commissary. Night after night from the time I was old enough to notice your eyes. Don't you know it nearly killed me? Made me insane?

FRAU VON PUSSENHEIMER. My point exactly. Forgive me. I was young then. I have come upon my method through much trial and error. Greta, you have until noon tomorrow.

MISS PHILLIPS. Ludmilla, please, the girls need me...

(They are interrupted by the girls crying out "Martha" offstage.)

MISS PHILLIPS. Martha!

(They exit. Blackout.)

Scene Eleven
Martha Is Dead

(The stage is in semidarkness. The girls hold candles and search for Martha.)

ALL. Martha! Martha!

THALIA. Martha! Please come quickly. Frau von Pussenheimer will be very upset if we are not in our beds. Martha, please!

MILLICENT. I saw the look in her eye. It gave me such a fright. So cold. She didn't even see me.

THALIA. I think I heard something.

DAMWELL & MILLICENT. Where?

THALIA. Behind the chest.

BABE. Ohhhh.

DAMWELL. Now what is it?

BABE. I'm still hungry and now I'm cold.

DAMWELL. I can't believe you're complaining at a time like this. We've got to find Martha.

ALL. Martha!

(The girls come downstage, facing the audience. The following lines should overlap slightly:)

MILLICENT. The water runs cool and dark and full of those weeds –

DAMWELL. I was sitting in the attic when the bells rang –

MILLICENT. Long, dark weeds: don't want to get tangled –

DAMWELL. I ran down the stairs as quickly as I could, just in time to see Dick at the edge of the grass with Babe and Millicent close behind –

MILLICENT. Next to a big, warm rock, I saw a foot. No one had to tell me it was Martha's –

BABE. I swam fast and I called Frau von Pussenheimer –

DAMWELL. He held you in his arms as if he didn't quite know how to hold you. As though carrying some dread message of some awful mistake –

MILLICENT. All white and puffy-looking, sickly yellow through the water –

BABE. I had a big duckweed caught in my hair. Frau von Pussenheimer was mad 'cause I was swimming in the river alone but she was crying too about Martha –

MILLICENT. "Clambering to hang, an envious sliver broke" –

DAMWELL. He put you on the dining room table. Will standing there all wet and trembling. Frau von Pussenheimer let us sit there and look at you while we waited for the coroner to come –

BABE. She was caught in those weeds like a guppy in a science room aquarium –

DAMWELL. I'd never seen you before without that crease in your forehead. You wore it even in your sleep. I'd never seen you sleep so peacefully –

WILL. In my heart I have already left. I am in it, Martha. Your leaving has pitched me right into the whole mess –

MILLICENT. Everyone must pray. Everyone must pray tonight. Everyone must pray for Martha's soul.

(They blow out their candles.)

Scene Twelve
Will Leaves

(**THALIA** *comes upon* **WILL** *in the root cellar;* **WILL** *is preparing to leave.*)

THALIA. Will!

WILL. Get out of here!

THALIA. They're looking all over for you! We all thought you were dead, too!

WILL. I wish I were. Get out, damn you!

THALIA. What are you doing?

WILL. What does it look like?

THALIA. You mean, you're going? Dressed like that?

WILL. Yes! Now get out! And you better not tell anyone you saw me down here!

THALIA. You're a bully! You've been nothing but a bully since I met you!

WILL. Sorry.

THALIA. I'll help you, if you want.

WILL. I don't need any help. I been out there before. I know my way around.

THALIA. You can't go like that. I mean, you want them to think you're a boy, don't you?

WILL. Why? I think I look like a boy pretty good.

THALIA. It's your hair. Wait here. I'll find a scissors.

WILL. No. Here. (*She produces her penknife.*) Cut it off. Cut it all off. I don't want it. I want to be somebody else. I'm gonna leave this place and never look back. Never.

THALIA. You won't miss your friends?

WILL. What? Who?

THALIA. Damwell. Millicent. Babe.

WILL. They're all right...I'm just different, that's all. I can't explain it. I belong out on the road where nobody knows me. I like people looking at me and they don't know who I am.

(THALIA cuts off WILL's ponytail.)

THALIA. There. You look good like this.

WILL. What're you gonna do?

THALIA. I don't know. I guess I'll just stay here. I'm not as rough as you.

WILL. Yeah. Well, I'll see you down the road, I guess.

THALIA. I guess. Good luck. You'd better go. The sun's coming up. You'd better go.

WILL. Thalia?

THALIA. Yeah?

WILL. Tell the others...tell them I said good-bye.

THALIA. I will. Run.

WILL. Thalia?

THALIA. Yes?

(WILL kisses THALIA.)

WILL. For good luck.

THALIA. For good luck.

(WILL leaves.)

Good luck, Will.

(She puts her fingers to her cheek remembering the kiss. Lights slowly fade on THALIA holding WILL's ponytail.)

Scene Thirteen
Frau von Pussenheimer's Farewell

*(*FRAU VON PUSSENHEIMER*'s office.)*

FRAU VON PUSSENHEIMER. Oh, this rage! Where can it go? Where can it go in these damp walls? I only wanted to shelter you. To keep you from the drooling men. And now I see that I cannot. They seep in through the cracks in the door. And now all my girls are leaving me. Beautiful Martha. Bold young Will. I've failed. Of course, I never could have succeeded. I cannot create a planet of women where there is no pain to little girls and only excessive pleasure for their growing bodies. Failing this, what is there for me? I will never turn to them. I will never concede. That would be to die over and over again one million times. It is better to die but once. *(She reveals a noose.)* Good-bye. Good-bye, my tender young buds, soon to be gorgeous flowers. May you protect yourselves better than I have.

(She hurls the noose over the rafters. Blackout.)

Scene Fourteen
Miss Phillips's Farewell

(The main hall. MISS PHILLIPS prepares to go. DAM-WELL and MILLICENT protest and whimper. THALIA carries MISS PHILLIPS's trunk.)

MISS PHILLIPS. Come now. Strong hearts. Brave smiles everyone.

MILLICENT. Miss Phillips, don't go.

DAMWELL. Don't leave us.

MISS PHILLIPS. Oh, girls. I must. You can't see it now, but there's a whole world out there waiting for you. I hope I have given you the tools you need to fashion it to your hearts' desires. Come. We must make an end of it.

(MISS PHILLIPS pushes MILLICENT and DAMWELL aside to have another deep kiss with THALIA. MISS PHILLIPS exits. Offstage she is heard knocking on FRAU VON PUSSENHEIMER's door. No answer. She knocks again.)

Frau von Pussenheimer?

(We hear her knock several times. She frantically tries to get the door open. Finally she pushes through.)

Ludmilla, please! Oh, Ludmilla! No!

(She screams and then comes staggering back, collapsing into the girls' arms.)

Girls. I'm afraid I have some bad news...and some good news!

(blackout)

ACT II

Scene One
Damwell's Wedding

(The grand ballroom of the Hôtel Goldene Gewölbe, Vienna, 1939. It is **DAMWELL***'s wedding day. Wedding music subsides into the sounds of the conversation and music of a reception.* **BABE**, **MILLICENT** *and* **THALIA** *are centerstage.* **MILLICENT** *is wearing the necklace of tears, which has noticeably increased in size.* **DAMWELL** *stands away from them, in her wedding dress.)*

DAMWELL. Thalia! Babe! Millicent!

(They turn and see **DAMWELL**. *They wave.)*

Well, we're on our way! Jean-Pierre is waiting.

(horn honks)

Just a minute, Jean-Pierre!
(to **THALIA**, **BABE** *and* **MILLICENT***)* There's just one more thing – catch!

(She throws her bouquet. No one makes a move to catch it. **THALIA**, **BABE** *and* **MILLICENT** *exchange looks.* **DAMWELL** *retrieves the bouquet.)*

Oh, well. Maybe I wasn't close enough. Let's try again. Ready? Catch!

(She throws it a second time; they each take a step back. **DAMWELL** *nervously giggles. She retrieves the bouquet again.)*

Come on, Millicent. I'm trying to do you a favor. You're not the prettiest of girls.

*(***DAMWELL** *throws the bouquet toward an insulted* **MIL-LICENT**, *who doesn't move a muscle.)*

DAMWELL. *(cont.)* Come on, Babe. For an old school friend. You'll help me out, won't you?

(**DAMWELL** *throws the bouquet again.* **BABE** *doesn't catch it.*)

Thalia will help me, won't you, Thalia? Come on. It's a tradition in my country. Catch it!

(**DAMWELL** *hurls the bouquet at* **THALIA**. **THALIA** *dodges it.* **DAMWELL** *chases* **THALIA** *around the stage, throwing the bouquet.*)

What? Did you all come just to eat the free food?! Catch it!

(blackout)

Scene Two
The Disembarkation

(New York Harbor, 1943. **BABE,** *with her companion, the* **BARONESS,** *has just arrived from overseas and is giving a press conference. The* **BARONESS** *holds* **BABE***'s dog,* **NIPPER** *[a hand puppet].)*

REPORTER #1. Babe! Babe! Was Nina Rostova any match for you on the green?

BABE. Nina's a wonderful friend and she gave me a run for my money!

REPORTER #2. Babe! Speaking of money, we understand you did pretty well today!

BABE. Well, let's just say it beats making soap at the orphanage!

REPORTER #1. What about Wimbledon, Babe? Any predictions on how you'll –

BABE. First things first, fellas. I gotta rest up for the Olympics tomorrow!

REPORTER #2. Hey, Babe! Who's your pretty friend?

(The **BARONESS** *and* **BABE** *exchange a look.)*

BABE. Uh...that's it for now, fellas.

REPORTER #1 & REPORTER #2. Ah, nuts!

(The **REPORTERS** *exit.)*

BARONESS. Come along, Babe.

MILLICENT. *(entering)* Excuse me. Excuse me.

BARONESS. No more questions. She is tired.

MILLICENT. I just want an autograph.

BARONESS. I said she is tired.

BABE. S'all right, Ginka. One autograph ain't gonna kill me. Who shall I make it out to, doll?

MILLICENT. To Millicent.

BABE. Millicent! *(to the* **BARONESS***)* Aw, look! It's my old pal, Millicent, from T-Puss!

BARONESS. *(disdainfully)* Pleased, I'm sure.

BABE. Millicent, this is my trusty companion, Nipper.

MILLICENT. *(mistaking the* **BARONESS** *for Nipper)* Why hello, Nipper.

BABE. How the heck are you, for god's sake! I haven't seen you since Damwell's wedding. Too bad about the divorce. Say, Millicent, you don't look so hot. I guess the world's not ready for a musical genius like yourself, huh?

MILLICENT. Actually, I'm pursuing a different career now, Babe. May I have a word with you, privately?

BABE. Sure, sure. *(to the* **BARONESS***)* Skunkers, do you mind? I'll only be a minute.

BARONESS. Well, all right. But make it quick. We have a train to catch in the morning.

BABE. Of course, my darling one.

(The **BARONESS** *makes kissing noises until* **BABE** *kisses her, then exits.)*

Women! So what's happening, Millicent? You look like a death sandwich warmed over.

MILLICENT. No, thanks. I wanted to see you, Babe. You're doing quite well for yourself, aren't you?

BABE. Isn't it grand? I've got all the money in the world. I travel like a king. The whole world adores me and best of all, I'm not a klutz anymore.

*(***BABE** *accidentally slams* **MILLICENT** *with* **MILLICENT***'s autograph book.)*

At least not on the playing field.

MILLICENT. You've grown up. Your great big hands and feet finally match your body a little. I'm so proud, Babe.

BABE. I never could've done it without all the girls at T-Puss. Especially you, Millicent. You were always the kindest and the most patient. All my success – I owe it to you.

MILLICENT. Then you wouldn't mind paying back a little of that patience and understanding?

BABE. Millicent, you name it.

MILLICENT. The world is changing very fast, Babe. Innocent people are going to be hurt. I've been trying to help these people in whatever way I can. But these are times that call for sacrifice. As Miss Phillips said to me – before the consumption took her on to heaven – she said, the world needs to be tended like a garden, and that I should be like a garden-tender. And sometimes to be a garden-tender you can't worry about yourself, you can only worry about the garden. She said this to me and she gave me the necklace of tears. Do you understand?

BABE. I guess so.

MILLICENT. Good. You're going to the Olympic games in Stockholm, yes?

BABE. You bet. I'm entered in rowing, dressage and gymnastics.

MILLICENT. I wondered if you would take a package for me to a friend. I'd rather not tell you anything more except that there's a chance you'll be caught and almost certainly be killed. Please think about it, Babe, would you? For an old school chum?

(**BABE** *nods her head nervously. Lights out.*)

Scene Three
Babe on a Plane

(The cockpit of the Grand Dame, a few weeks later. **BABE** *flies the plane with Nipper by her side.)*

BABE. Well, Nipper, looks like it's just you and me and the Axis. I always feel calm up here, Nips, don't you? Dropping that package for my old pal, Millicent, sure made me feel young again. Like I have something to give the world. Like my days back at T-Puss on the hockey field. I could've done anything and now I have. I've done something real for the first time in my life, Nips. Oh sure, I know. I made folks happy when I broke the land speed record; gave them all something to cheer about. But it was always so empty, Nipper. Heck. I don't have to tell you that. You were with me all the way in Death Valley, you know how I felt about it. Yeah, Nipper – I don't know where all this is headed, but when that pine lid comes down they're gonna say that Deirdre "Babe" O'Hanlon did something for humanity. Aw, don't cry, Nipper. I hate it when you get all emotional...

(Nipper whimpers.)

Nipper? What is it, girl?

(Nipper barks.)

Package?

(Barks again.)

What other package?

(Barks out of control.)

OK. Don't get so excited. Bring it up here, we'll see what it is.

(Nipper ducks into the cockpit.)

I'm sure it's not that important –

(Nipper reappears with a bomb in her mouth.)

BABE. *(cont.)* NUTS! Nipper! That's a bomb. OK, Nips – drop it.

(Nipper refuses.)

Nipper, drop the ball-y.

(Nipper refuses again.)

I'm not playin' here, Nipper, DROP IT! NIPPER!

(Lights out as we hear the plane going down. Explosion.)

Scene Four
Vin's Place

(On the street, outside a gay Parisian nightclub – Vin Marconi's – 1946.)

THALIA. This dirty street. Why are we always relegated to the filthiest street in the most abhorrent part of town? I feel lost. I hope I got the directions correctly. I think she said Rue de la Quare. But I cannot be sure. Something has pulled me here tonight. The same thing that has pulled me my whole life – through the interrogation and over the Alps on foot. What is it? A smile? A promise from someone long ago forgotten? Of happiness? That someday I will rest in a pair of strong arms holding me? I delude myself. I hope and my hopes are dashed.

(She knocks on the door of the nightclub. A peephole opens.)

PIERRE. *(through the peephole)* Qu'est-ce que vous voulez?

THALIA. "I'm sure the baguette is stale."

(The door opens.)

PIERRE. Ah! Bienvenue, mademoiselle. Right this way.

*(**THALIA** enters and is seated at a table. Drum roll.)*

Merci, mes dames et mes dames. Et maintenant, I bring to you the most wonderful, the one, the only, Vin Marconi!

*(Applause. **WILL** appears in drag à la Marlene Dietrich in Morocco.)*

WILL. *(singing "Vin Marconi's Song" in a French accent)*
I'VE ALWAYS LOVED THE GIRLS
I DON'T KNOW WHY, I DON'T KNOW WHY
I WANT TO KISS THE GIRLS
AND NOT THE GUYS, NO, NOT THE GUYS.

THIS PUZZLED ME WHEN I WAS YOUNGER
AND, OH, HOW I DID WONDER
HOW COULD I APPEASE THIS BURNING HUNGER?

WILL. *(cont.)*

AND THEN I MET HER
I SHAN'T FORGET HER
SHE TOLD ME SHE COULD LOVE ME SO I LET HER
AND HOW OUR LOVE DID GROW
SHE TAUGHT ME ALL I KNOW
HAND IN HAND ALONG THE SEINE
PROVING TO ME I WAS A LESBIAN.

BUT LONG IT COULD NOT LAST
SHE LOVED ME DEEP
SHE LOVED ME FAST
I AWOKE ONE MORNING TO FIND HER GONE
I HAD TO FIND A REASON TO GO ON.

AND THEN I MET THEM
I SHAN'T FORGET THEM
I LOVED THEM ONE AND ALL
WHEN I COULD GET THEM
IN THE VAST PARADE OF STARS
WE WERE SO YOUNG, THE WORLD WAS OURS
WE WERE SO GAY, IN EVERY WAY
CAROUSING WITH THE FLOTSAM AND THE JETSAM.

BUT AS THE YEARS ROLL CRUELLY BY,
WITH COUNTLESS LOVES AND COUNTLESS SAD GOOD-BYES
THE MIRROR TELLS ME TRUTHFULLY I'VE GROWN
I PLAN TO LIVE MY LATER YEARS ALONE.

(to **THALIA***)* AND THEN I SAW YOU
HOW I ADORE YOU
WHEN YOU FIX YOUR HAIR
I WANT TO DO IT FOR YOU
IS THIS TRUE LOVE AT LAST?
HOW I'M AFRAID TO ASK.

MY KNEES ARE WEAK
I CANNOT SPEAK
I TOOK THE STAGE
BLOOD'S BOILING RAGE.

IS THIS TRUE LOVE
OR IS IT JUST OLD AGE?

*(Applause. **WILL** exits, then reenters with a champagne bottle and two glasses.)*

WILL. *(cont.)* Hello. May I join you? I only sing in that accent. I'm Vin Marconi.

THALIA. I know.

WILL. Who are you?

THALIA. I'm not sure. I think I'm starting to remember. Your song was very...amusing.

WILL. I'm afraid I'm an awful coward. I can never say just what I mean.

THALIA. What do you mean?

WILL. Shall we have a drink? Champagne.

THALIA. This is my first time.

WILL. At a nightclub?

THALIA. At this particular kind of nightclub. Where I've been, they don't have these kind of clubs. It's hard enough just to survive, let alone have a little fun. Paris is a great relief.

WILL. Times are hard all over – for everybody. I hate being careful. Tonight, to hell with being careful!

THALIA. I'll drink to that. Vin Marconi. That's an unusual name.

WILL. It's not mine, but in a way it is. You see, years back I was in the war. I disguised myself as a man and drove an ambulance. I saw a lot of action. One time, during some pretty heavy shelling, I ran into a young soldier. He was hurt pretty bad...

*(Flashback. Sound of bombing and gunfire. **WILL** and a soldier (**VIN**) smack into each other downstage. **WILL** cradles the dying soldier.)*

Hey, fella, you're hurt pretty bad. I'll go get a medic...

VIN. Forget it, kid, those krauts got us pinned down pretty good.

WILL. But you're bleeding, I'm just an ambulance driver –

VIN. Listen, kid. I'm just about to buy the farm and I need ya here with me. There's just something about you, kid, you remind me of a friend of mine. I got his picture. Want to see it?

WILL. Sure.

VIN. *(pulls out dog tags with a locket attached)* He's real sweet looking, ain't he? Fellas woulda give me the business if they knew his picture was in there. Harold. Not Harry neither. Harold. Ain't that a sophisticated name? Don't know what he ever saw in a bum like me.

WILL. I'm sure he loves you very much.

VIN. You keep it, kid. Keep the whole thing.

WILL. But, you're not gonna die! I'm gonna help you!

VIN. You're a real pal, kid. A good fella. Just sit quiet with me. Until the fighting stops. *(dies)*

WILL. No! Hold on! Don't die! Come on, pal...don't die. I don't even know your name. *(looks at tags)* Vin Marconi...

*(**WILL** drops **VIN**. The flashback ends. **WILL** crosses back to table)*

So you see, I figured it was the least I could do for him.

THALIA. What a terrible story. Sometimes it feels like this whole world's gone crazy. Sometimes I feel crazy. I don't feel crazy tonight. You make me feel so calm, a little excited too. I feel as if you're reading me like a book, Vin Marconi.

WILL. I know you. I knew you from the very first moment I saw you – so frightened but not showing it. I talked a good game, but I never coulda made it out that cellar window if you hadn't pushed me.

THALIA. Will.

WILL. That's right, Thalia.

THALIA. I knew there was some reason –

WILL. I've been waiting for you, Thalia. Since that cold, gray morning ten years ago. Your smile, your courage. I never could've left Tilue-Pussenheimer without them. I never could've left behind the memory of Martha.

THALIA. Oh, Will. You loved her.

WILL. Yes. But now I love you.

(**THALIA** *gasps.*)

Relax. I don't expect you to fall into my arms. After all these years and so much water under the –

(**THALIA** *interrupts* **WILL** *with a kiss.*)

THALIA. I do love you. I've always loved you.

WILL. Then Paris is ours! There's been so much sorrow, so much suffering in our short lives. It's all over now, my darling. There will be no more crack of Frau von P's boot horn to frighten us. No more kisses stolen in the hayloft. No more words unspoken. Our love will parade down the streets of Paris! I will write you poems on the front page of *Le Monde*! I will marry you in Notre Dame! I will sing your name every night, my darling!

THALIA. Yes, Will. Let's begin at once. I was so tired. And now I see what has tired me – the hiding, the lies, the fear of being found out. When I was crossing the Alps, my feet frozen in my cheap cardboard shoes, there were so many moments when all I wanted was to lie down and pull the snow over me like a blanket of death, and sleep. Something, the smallest, most quiet voice urged me onward. Onward, I think, to you.

(*They go to kiss.*)

PIERRE. (*offstage*) Vin! You must sign for the linen!

WILL. The mundane world comes crashing in. I won't be but a moment, my angel! (*exits*)

THALIA. To feel the air in my lungs. To take a drink of champagne and not be afraid to let it go to my head. Why not? The champagne tastes divine!

(*The sound of a truck backing up. Screams and exclamations are heard offstage. Crashing noises.* **PIERRE** *drags* **WILL**'s *mangled body halfway onstage.*)

PIERRE. She's been run over by the delivery truck! She is dead!

THALIA. No. No. It cannot be! Will, my love, my heart, my soul. Will, please don't leave me again. I can't bear it. Choke me! Choke me! Oh! This life of sorrows! This life of never-ending sorrows! *(stumbles to the table, picks up a bottle)* To your health! *(drinks)*

(blackout)

Scene Five
The Rehearsal

(A Broadway theatre, 1956. Rehearsal for a production of a play directed by **DAMWELL***. The sound of rain comes up in the dark. Lights come up on a chair, center, where* **AUDREY** *[playing the role of Sharon] sits, forlorn.* **SHIRLEY** *[playing the role of Bertha] stands just downstage left, looking out into the audience. The actors hold their scripts loosely in their hands. These characters should be reminiscent of Shirley MacLaine and Audrey Hepburn playing Martha and Karen in Lillian Hellman's play* The Children's Hour.*)*

SHIRLEY. Where's Guy gone off to?

AUDREY *(as if awakening from a dream)* Pardon?

SHIRLEY. Guy. His car just pulled away. Dinner's almost ready.

AUDREY. He won't be joining us.

SHIRLEY. Not another emergency, I hope. He's too good. Always taking care of everyone else, never a worry for himself.

AUDREY. Hmmmm.

SHIRLEY. I'll keep his supper warm. He'll need a good, warm meal when he gets back.

AUDREY. *(in a sudden burst of anguish)* Oh, Guy!

SHIRLEY. *(quickly walks to* **AUDREY***)* What is it, Sharon? Is something wrong?

AUDREY. Everything is wrong.

SHIRLEY. Was it something I said? Something I did?

AUDREY. No, Bertha.

SHIRLEY. What then?

(no answer)

What? Tell me, Sharon. What?

AUDREY. It's not you, Bertha. It's Guy. He thought that you and I...Oh, I can't say it. It's all so dirty and filthy.

SHIRLEY. But I thought he knew. He *knew* it was all a lie. How could he believe that we –

AUDREY. He doesn't know what to believe anymore. Do you?

SHIRLEY. It's all my fault.

AUDREY. Oh, Bertha. Don't talk like that.

SHIRLEY. It is me, isn't it? All this talk. All this trouble. All because of me.

AUDREY. Bertha, that's not true.

SHIRLEY. You're a good friend, Sharon. A loving friend. You and Guy are made for each other. Always looking out for other people, never a thought for yourselves. I want you to be together. I've always wanted it. Go to him now. I'm sure it's not too late.

AUDREY. What's done is done. There's no changing it.

SHIRLEY. It's no use going on like this. I'll pack my bags. I can be out of here first thing tomorrow. I've been so selfish. Now I see it. Don't worry, Sharon. I won't stand in your way.

AUDREY. Bertha! What are you talking about?

SHIRLEY. Don't you see?

AUDREY. See what? I *can't* see it. I *refuse* to see it. Why should we let a nasty little lie come between us? If you leave, I'm going with you.

SHIRLEY. But that only makes it worse. People will think it's really true.

AUDREY. Who cares anymore what people think?

SHIRLEY. Besides, there isn't anywhere for us to go. This lie will follow us to the ends of the earth. In every city, every town, we'll be ridiculed and scorned.

AUDREY. There must be someplace where people can sort lies from the truth.

SHIRLEY. No. There's no escaping this. Not for me. Save yourself, Sharon.

AUDREY. Nonsense. You're talking nonsense. *(She approaches* **SHIRLEY.***)*

SHIRLEY. No! Don't touch me.

AUDREY. *(stopping dead in her tracks)* Bertha, please. Surely you and I know the difference between an innocent touch and an illicit act.

SHIRLEY. Do we?

AUDREY. Don't talk crazy. Of course we do.

SHIRLEY. A little girl tells a lie. Why does she tell a lie? She says she saw something. But what did she see? There's nothing to see. Unless she sees something we're not seeing.

AUDREY. What can you be saying?

SHIRLEY. *(finally breaking down)* Oh, god! Strike me down now! Take me before I can sin anymore! Even while we've been talking I can't stop thinking about how much I love you. I am what they say. Cursed and wretched. An abomination. More filthy and dirty than you could ever imagine.

*(**AUDREY** runs to **SHIRLEY** and takes her in her arms. Shirley's character, Bertha, is too overcome with grief and shame to resist.)*

AUDREY. Bertha. Bertha, please. Stop it.

*(**SHIRLEY** looks up to **AUDREY** as **AUDREY** gently caresses **SHIRLEY**'s face.)*

I can't believe these things I'm hearing.

SHIRLEY. Believe it. It's all true. Finally, we come to the horrible truth.

AUDREY. *(looking at the script)* It's not so horrible. Now that I think about it, it sounds pretty good. Come on, baby. Rub me. Rub on me, baby. Let me be a prostrate worshipper in your grotto of love. Oh yeah. Hump me, you...you...lascivious Jezebel. *(She stares at her script, incredulous.)* Is this right?

SHIRLEY. *(showing **AUDREY** in the script)* I think it's "grotto of *moist* love."

AUDREY. Did Lillian write this?

*(**DAMWELL** enters through the audience.)*

DAMWELL. People! People! Please! Audrey. Shirley. What is the problem here? We had some momentum going. Now let's take it back to, "Rub on me, baby." OK? And...lights up.

AUDREY. Damwell, this is not Lillian's writing.

DAMWELL. I don't know what to tell you, Audrey. That's what she gave me.

AUDREY. But this is your handwriting. You've crossed out all of her lines and written in lines of your own.

DAMWELL. OK. OK. Just between the three of us, I'm helping her out. She was shit-faced when she wrote this – it's crap. I'm just perking it up a little. No one needs to be the wiser.

AUDREY. But you're changing the whole intention! Sharon never would have said these things.

SHIRLEY. That's right, Miss Maxwell. Didn't Lillian say the whole point of the story was about how lies can hurt people? I mean, they're not really inverts.

AUDREY. Oh, I never would have agreed to play an invert.

DAMWELL. Is there a doctor in the house? Emergency! Miss Hepburn needs the pole removed from her butt! Miss Hepburn needs a polectomy!

AUDREY. That's it! I quit! I'm going to call that nice Capote man and tell him I'm available for that breakfast movie! *(She storms off.)*

DAMWELL. What? You afraid you're gonna catch something from Shirley!?

SHIRLEY. Ooooh! Take another Seconal, why don't you! *(also storms off)*

DAMWELL. *(calling after her)* You'll be back!

SHIRLEY. *(offstage)* Not in this lifetime, lady!

DAMWELL. Fine. Fine. I don't need any of you. Actor-types! Writer-types! Huh! Reds! Reds and alcoholics, the lot of you. *(taking out pills and eating them)* Right! Like I'm the only muff-diver in this crowd. I don't think so. You can't blame me for talking. There's a scourge upon the land. There's a scourge...Isn't there?

(blackout)

Scene Six
The Mission

(A mission on the Bowery, New York City, 1959. MIL-
LICENT *is cutting a large carrot into a soup pot. She is
wearing the necklace of tears, which is even bigger than
before.)*

MILLICENT. *(singing to herself to the tune of "Turtles Are Free")*
WHEN AN AVIATOR DIES
AND A PRETTY, YOUNG RESISTANCE FIGHTER CRIES
AND THE WORLD IS CHANGED FOREVER –

(spoken) Oh, Babe. How could I ever have sent you off
to such a wretched death? I don't deserve the cup of
watery pea soup I eat daily. I am wretched. Horrible. I
don't deserve my miserable cot.

*(*THALIA *enters, singing drunkenly to the tune of Vin
Marconi's song:)*

THALIA.
AND THEN I MET HER
AND THEN I MET HER
AND THEN I MET HER AND I MET HER AND I MET HER.

(spoken) All right, I'm here. What do I do now? Confess? I confess. I confess everything.

MILLICENT. *(still working over her pot)* This is not a church.
It's a mission. You may speak to god here if you like.
All we ask is that you leave the evil alcohol devil out-
side.

THALIA. Millicent?

MILLICENT. Yes…

THALIA. Hahahahaha!

MILLICENT. What's so funny?

THALIA. Do the words Tilue-Pussenheimer mean anything
to you?

MILLICENT. Oh my god. Here, why don't you lie down on
this cot –

THALIA. *(singing to the tune of "The T-Puss Fight Song")*
OOOOOH! WHO'S THE BRAVEST SMILER!
AT TILUE-PUSSENHEIMER!
IT'S ME, IT'S ME, IT'S ME!
I'M A FILTHY DRUNK!

MILLICENT. Thalia, please!

THALIA. Funny, isn't it. Ol' von P. always said, "Don't pick on Thalia. At least Thalia will never become a stinking drunk. Her people never become stinking drunks." Proved the old bitch wrong, I guess. You're a brave smiler, aren'tcha?

*(***THALIA*** collapses. Blackout.)*

(Lights up. A banner reading "Three Days Later" is held up from offstage.)

MILLICENT. Oh, lord. Why have you sent her here? I came here to serve my penance, lord! For my sins and my evil thoughts! Remember? I asked you to keep me far, far away from women – with their fleshy calves and shapely hips and...Oh, lord, I'm trouble, don't you see? Trouble with a capital T! Please, god, I feel bad saying this, but, please, if you care about me at all, let her be in a coma and never wake up.

THALIA. Oh, my head!

MILLICENT. Oh, god! There is no god!

THALIA. Millicent! How long have I been asleep?

MILLICENT. About three days. You certainly slept like the dead. Well, g'bye now!

THALIA. Can't I stay with you a moment? I don't feel quite right...

MILLICENT. I think it'd be better if you just went on your way. I've got a lot of hungry bums to feed, you see, and...

THALIA. Forgive me, Millicent.

MILLICENT. You? Forgive you? Why, how silly. I'm the one who should ask for forgiveness really –

THALIA. I was drunk.

MILLICENT. Yes, a little.

THALIA. When I was sleeping, sometimes I awoke to see you looking down at me – caring for me – your eyes so blue and full of light. Millicent, you are an angel –

MILLICENT. I wasn't staring at you! Now, really, I think you should be going.

THALIA. Your necklace. It's so beautiful. Where did you get it?

MILLICENT. You don't want to know.

THALIA. I do. It's lovely.

MILLICENT. Here! You can have it. I don't want it anymore. Take it and all that goes with it. She gave it to me, Thalia. Miss Phillips!

THALIA. Oh, Millicent. My life is bleak. I have crawled into a bottle of scotch and I cannot get out. You rehabilitate here, don't you? Rehabilitate me, Millicent! Please!

MILLICENT. No! I don't rehabilitate! I just serve soup! And I'm not even very good at that! Ask anyone! They all hate my soup! You don't get it, do you, Thalia? I'm poison! Poison with a capital P! If you know what's good for you, you'll flee! As fast as you can.

THALIA. Very well. I'm going. I know somewhere I can go. It was good to see you again, Millicent.

(THALIA *goes to leave. Music swells and she sings "Thalia's Lament":*)

THERE'S A BRAVE SMILE LOOKING BACK AT ME
IT REMINDS ME OF THE GIRL I USED TO BE
ONCE I HAD A HEART BUT I GUESS I BROKE IT
ONCE I HAD A SONG BUT NOW I CHOKE ON IT.

AND OUTSIDE THE SNOW IS FALLING
LIKE MY TEARS ONLY FROZEN
AND I CAN'T TURN AWAY FROM THIS LONELY PATH
I'VE CHOSEN.

IN THE WARMTH OF A BAR
A STEADY HAND TO HOLD
SO TONIGHT, JUST FOR TONIGHT,
LET ME NOT BE ALONE.

(**THALIA** *goes to leave.*)

MILLICENT. Thalia, wait! Stay with me! I will help you. Only you've got to help me, too. Help me to let go of the past.

THALIA. I will try.

MILLICENT. Oh! Smell the air! Thalia, it's spring! A time of new beginnings. We're going to start all fresh, Thalia. We're getting out of the Bowery. I know there's not much money, but we can take a small apartment somewhere, in a humble neighborhood where rents are low. I'll help you stop drinking and you can help me write that book of poetry I've been meaning to write for so many years. Yes! Our life will be beautiful and lovely and nobody, nobody, nobody will ever be able to spoil it! Oh, Thalia, I'm happy.

(*They go to kiss. A* **BUM** *enters, brandishing a knife.*)

BUM. Hey! Sister! Gimme all your money!

THALIA. Millicent, look out!

MILLICENT. It's all right, Thalia. We have no money here, sir. We're an operation of the lord. We have a bowl of hot soup if that interests you.

BUM. I don't want your soup! I want your money!

MILLICENT. I tell you, we haven't any money.

BUM. If you haven't got any money, then maybe there's something else I can have. (*leering at* **THALIA**) Who's your pretty friend?

MILLICENT. You leave her alone.

BUM. You're awful pretty.

MILLICENT. You touch her and I'll...I'll kill you.

BUM. (*laughs*) What are ya gonna do? Kill me with that book?!

(**MILLICENT** *whacks the* **BUM** *with her diary. He collapses, dead.*)

THALIA. Millicent!

MILLICENT. My poems are deadly.

(*blackout*)

Scene Seven
I Want to Live

(Sing Sing Prison, October 12, 1959, 11:59 p.m. The style is atmospheric, noir. The sound of sirens and the clang of a prison door is heard in the blackout. The lights come up. MILLICENT is seen handcuffed and smoking nervously.)

MILLICENT. It was an accident, I tell you! Haven't you ever heard of self-defense? I want to live! I want to live!

(blackout)

Scene Eight
The Book Signing

(A book signing at Rizzoli bookstore in New York City, 1969. **DAMWELL** *is signing copies of her best-selling autobiography.)*

DAMWELL. And what's your name, darling? Kitty? Grrrrowwwl! *(She signs a book.)* "To Kitty. Best of luck, Damwell Maxwell." Thanks so much for coming. Hello! How are you? And your name is...Richard! Handsome name, handsome fellow. Yes...I hope you enjoy it. Thanks so much for coming.

*(***THALIA*** enters. She is wearing the necklace of tears.)*

Next?

THALIA. Perhaps you could sign one for me?

DAMWELL. That's what I'm here for. And your name is – Thalia? Oh, my goodness. Look everyone! It's Thalia! From Tilue-Pussenheimer! Chapter three! The tiny, little Hebrew girl! Oh my! How are you?

THALIA. I'm well, Damwell. You...you're a famous author now. What a life you've had. I've seen all your pictures.

DAMWELL. Oh, that was so long ago.

THALIA. My favorite one was *Two Planes Over Morocco.* Yes. That was my favorite.

DAMWELL. Oh yes, well, I think I really captured the role of the nurse in that one, don't you? I –

*(***THALIA*** collapses.)*

Thalia? Thalia! Would someone please get me a glass of water! Oh, dear. You'll be all right, Thalia. I'll take you to my house in Southampton for a little while. The salt air will be just the thing. Taxi!

(blackout)

Scene Nine
Southampton

(DAMWELL's beach house in Southampton, later that day. DAMWELL is drinking a highball.)

DAMWELL. Are you feeling better, dear?

THALIA. Yes, thank you, Damwell.

DAMWELL. You gave me quite a fright. What's wrong with you, anyway, dear? Do you have a condition?

THALIA. You're very kind. But really, my life story is too horrible to share. I don't want to burden you.

DAMWELL. Oh, but you must. It's just the thing to make you feel better. Why, when I was in the mental hospital, Dr. LeFarge couldn't emphasize enough the importance of disclosure.

THALIA. You were in the mental hospital?

DAMWELL. Oh, for Pete's sake – haven't you read my book? Why, yes! You see, after I was blacklisted by that awful Senator Hungwell and the rest of them, well, my whole life simply went flush down the toilet. It seems that hideous Dick Moorehead – you remember Dick – was taking perverted photographs of myself and Tina – you remember Tina, the sophomore? And, well, there went my second marriage. Then they marched right in and took my lovely twins, Janey and Junie, and sent them to a state home. Well, it was all a bit much for me and I began, you know, wearing my nightgown and slippers in public, things like that. Fortunately, Dr. LeFarge and all the wonderful staff at Meadow Pines had me right as rain in just twelve years. Well, I'm not complaining. It gave me plenty of time to write my book: *I, Damwell Maxwell.* And as you saw, it's just a raving success.

THALIA. It must have taken tremendous personal courage to endure such hardship. I'm afraid we all misjudged you back at Tilue-Pussenheimer.

DAMWELL. Thanks. Now. You look like you could use a li'l scotch and soda. How 'bout that?

THALIA. No!

DAMWELL. Hold the soda?

THALIA. Uh...

DAMWELL. Maybe this'll loosen your tongue a little. Remember: disclosure.

(DAMWELL *hands* THALIA *her drink.* THALIA *sucks it down.*)

THALIA. Well, you see, after Will got run over by the delivery truck...

DAMWELL. Oh, my god!

THALIA. Yes. I thought I'd never love again. Then, I met Millicent. You remember Millicent.

DAMWELL. Oh, yes. The ethereal one. Always strumming on that awful guitar.

THALIA. Yes, Damwell. I met Millicent in a mission for wayward alcoholics. We fell in love. She gave me Miss Phillips's necklace of tears.

DAMWELL. Oh, how nice for you.

THALIA. Yes. And, well, you must know she was on death row for murdering a bum. Damwell, they gave her the electric chair. My life is one horrible tragedy after another. I don't know how I stand it.

DAMWELL. Oh, there, there now. Come on. Hey, hey, hey. What did they teach us back at the academy, Thalia, hmm?

(DAMWELL *mushes* THALIA*'s face into a brave smile.*)

Brave smiles! That's right. Brave smiles. *(smiling bravely)* See? How do you think I've gotten through the relentless tragedy that's been my life? It's not just the antidepressants, let me tell you. Look at me, Thalia. I'm free. I've got all the money in the world and my book is a smash.

THALIA. Oh, Damwell. I'm starting to feel all warm and tingly.

DAMWELL. See? What did I tell you? Let me make you another. Say, Thalia – let's put a record on the hi-fi and do some dance impressions, just like we used to at the academy!

(Wild, 1950s cha-cha music swells.)

THALIA. Oh, I couldn't possibly.

DAMWELL. From now on, "I couldn't possibly," will not be in your vocabulary. Come on!

*(*DAMWELL *pulls* THALIA *up. They dance through the end of the scene.)*

Isn't it lovely to feel so free and gay? Just like when we were girls!

THALIA. Yes! I do feel gay. I feel light!

DAMWELL. Thalia, I'm gonna help you. I'm gonna help you write your very own book.

THALIA. Me?

DAMWELL. Why not? With all the tragedy you've had? It's certain to be a bestseller! Your very own autobiography. Let's see...we'll call it...Necklace of Tears!

(blackout)

Scene Ten
Southampton

(Southampton, two years later. A banner reading "Two Years Later" appears from offstage. THALIA still wears the necklace of tears, which is now huge.)

THALIA. You shallow bitch! You empty publicity whore!

DAMWELL. Thalia, please! You've got to stop drinking!

THALIA. Why? Why would I stop the one thing in this life that gives me pleasure?!

DAMWELL. Don't I...aren't I some consolation to you, my darling –

THALIA. Yes, Damwell. You are the consolation prize!

DAMWELL. All right! Just give me that goddamn necklace!

THALIA. Mine, mine, mine, mine, mine! These are my tears and you can't have them!

DAMWELL. It's not my fault that you are too drunk to go on *The Mike Douglas Show* to promote the book! It's not my fault that I have to go on instead of you and I'm going to wear the goddamn necklace!

THALIA. You're jealous, Damwell. That's what you are! A pathetic, washed-up celebrity has-been! You're jealous because *Necklace of Tears* outsold *I, Damwell Maxwell*! Now Thalia is the star! Thalia is who they want! Damwell can go and be on the games shows!

DAMWELL. My god, Thalia! What's happened to us! We used to love each other! We used to be so good for each other...

(The phone rings.)

THALIA. Who is that? One of your fucking girlfriends?

DAMWELL. SHUT UP! WOULD YOU PLEASE SHUT UP FOR ONE MINUTE! *(answering the phone)* Helloo?

THALIA. If that's Mike Douglas, you tell him I'm not here!

DAMWELL. Yes, this is Damwell Maxwell.

THALIA. Slut!

DAMWELL. Oh yes. Yes, I've been waiting for your call.

THALIA. I'm queen of the house! I'm the queen.

DAMWELL. Yes? Yes? Oh no. No. I – it can't be. Yes. Thank you, Doctor.

THALIA. Who is that? Another one of your fucking doctor girlfriends?

DAMWELL. Thalia... *(She begins to cry.)*

THALIA. Oh, now she's crying. Boo hoo hoo. Poor little miss rich girl is crying her eyeballs out. Always feeling sorry for herself.

DAMWELL. We're gonna have to add another bead to the necklace of tears...

THALIA. You get your paws off my neckla – what do you mean?

DAMWELL. Oh Thalia. It's so horrible.

THALIA. What? What is so horrible? What could possibly be more horrible than our lives?

DAMWELL. Oh honey. You know those mood swings you've been having? And the headaches?

THALIA. Ya...

DAMWELL.....And, you know this big lump on the back of your head?

THALIA. I've been drinking a lot.

DAMWELL. It's not the drinking, Thalia.

THALIA. What is it?

DAMWELL. You have a malignant brain tumor.

THALIA. FUCK!...Maybe we can put it in the book.

DAMWELL. Good idea! You can be an inspiration to others with brain tumors –

THALIA. Yeah, and you can make some more money off me!

DAMWELL. Thalia...

THALIA. Get offa me.

DAMWELL. I always loved you so much.

THALIA. Oh shit, I'm gonna die.

DAMWELL. No, Thalia, no. Look outside the window, darling. Look how beautiful it is outside. Look at the seagulls, look at –

*(*THALIA *falls in a faint.)*

Oh my god!! They didn't say it was going to happen now!

*(*THALIA *mumbles.)*

Oh thank god. Don't die. I love you so much. *(pounds on her)* Goddamnit! Don't die! Don't die on me, you bastard! Thalia. I never thought I would be the one to survive. I thought I was the spoiled rich one who would just fall apart under the least bit of strain. Oh, please don't let me be the only one left!

THALIA. Mother...Mother...I see you, Mother.

DAMWELL. How can you see your mother? You're an orphan.

THALIA. Flowers...lovely white flowers...

DAMWELL. Oh, yes, lovely white flowers...

THALIA. I'll pick them, Muti. I'll get them. I'll pick them, Muti. Muti? The soldiers are coming, Muti.

DAMWELL. *(fiercely whispering to the imaginary soldiers)* Stay back!

THALIA. Muti? Muti?

(pause)

Damwell?

DAMWELL. Yes, I'm here, darling.

(During the following, as each name is mentioned, the dead orphans enter to form a sad and noble tableau.)

THALIA. Will?

DAMWELL. Well...

THALIA. Babe?

DAMWELL. Oh, yes, she's here.

THALIA. Millicent?

DAMWELL. Yes. Hi. Millicent's right here.

THALIA. Who's the bravest smiler?

DAMWELL. You are, honey!

THALIA. All the little orphan girls have gone to heaven. We're all little angels in the sky now. Finally happy. Finally free to live and to love. Real life begins now. *(She dies.)*

DAMWELL. *(wailing)* Thalia!

(fade to black)

The Tragic End

TURTLES ARE FREE

Words and music by Peg Healey

Oh, a tur-tle dies   and a young girl cries   the world is changed for-e-ver ...   When the death knell rings   Oh, the grief! It brings both tur-tle and girl   to-geth-er. ___   Tur-tles are ___ free Tur-tles   are ___   free   Tur-tles   are ___   free Oh, a tur-tle's life   is a hard, hard life . . .

THE T-PUSS FIGHT SONG

Words by The Five Lesbian Brothers
Music by Maureen Angelos

Ohhhh   who's   the heav - est smo - ker   at Ti - lus-Puss - en-hai - mer?   It's   Tha - lia, Tha - lia, Tha - lia ___   She's a   great big doll   But ___   we   love her an - y-way. Oh,

BRAVE SMILES

Words and music by Peg Healey

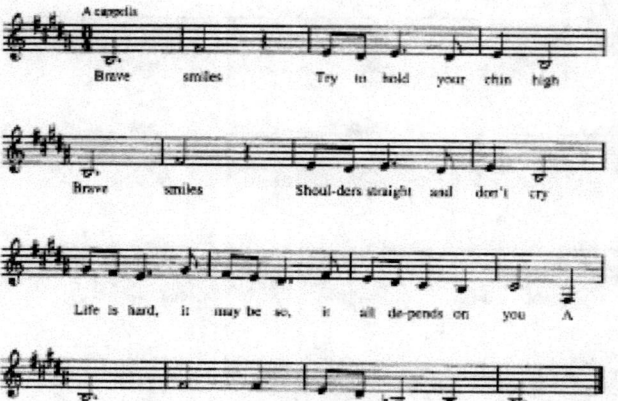

VIN MARCONI'S SONG

*Words and music by Peg Healey
and Dominique Dibbell*

THALIA'S LAMENT

Words and music by Dominique Dibbell

ABOUT THE FIVE LESBIAN BROTHERS

The Five Lesbian Brothers are Maureen Angelos, Babs Davy, Dominique Dibbell, Peg Healey, and Lisa Kron. The Brothers came together as a theater company in 1989 after performing together in various other combinations at the Obie award–winning WOW Cafe Theatre in New York City's East Village.

Together the Brothers have written five plays, *Voyage to Lesbos* (1990), *Brave Smiles* (1992), *The Secretaries* (1994), *Brides of the Moon* (1996), and *Oedipus at Palm Springs* (2006), which was written by Maureen Angelos, Dominique Dibbell, Peg Healey, and Lisa Kron.

The Brothers' work has been presented Off-Broadway and Off-Off Broadway by New York Theatre Workshop, the Joseph Papp Public Theatre, the WOW Cafe Theatre, Downtown Art Company, Performance Space 122, Dixon Place, La Mama, the Kitchen, and the Whitney Museum of American Art at Phillip Morris. They have toured to London, Los Angeles, San Francisco, San Diego, Houston, Columbus, Seattle, Philadelphia, Boston, and the deep woods of Michigan. Their plays have also been produced by other companies throughout the United States and, believe it or not, in Zagreb, Croatia.

The Brothers are the recipients of a Village Voice Obie Award, a New York Dance and Performance Award ("Bessie"), a GLAAD Media Award, and a New York Press Award as Best Performance Group. An anthology of their plays entitled *Five Lesbian Brothers/Four Plays* was published in 2000 by Theatre Communications Group and was nominated for a Lambda Literary award.

Also by
The Five Lesbian Brothers...

Brides of the Moon

Oedipus at Palm Springs

The Secretaries

Voyage to Lesbos

OTHER TITLES AVAILABLE FROM SAMUEL FRENCH

OEDIPUS AT PALM SPRINGS

The Five Lesbian Brothers
Maureen Angelos, Babs Davy, Dominique Dibbell, Peg
Healey and Lisa Kron

Comedic Tragedy / 5f

Irreverent theater group The Five Lesbian Brothers get their greasy prints on a classic. *Oedipus at Palm Springs* follows the dark adventure of two couples on a retreat to the desert resort town. While new parents Fran and Con try desperately to jump-start their sex life, May-December love bunnies Prin and Terri can't keep their hands off each other. What begins as a hilarious, boozey weekend takes a horrific turn after a secret is revealed. Two parts comedy with a shot of tragedy shaken over ice, *Oedipus at Palm Springs* is a brave examination of the messy guts of relationships.

"Along the way to the inevitable dark twist is much lightness and enlightenment to revel in–not just a lot of zingy one-liners about commitment, gay life in America, parenthood, and growing older, but also a real sense of these four women as women, friends, and lovers…. It may be the saddest comedy you'll ever see.
– *The Boston Globe*

"Richly funny as it is, *Oedipus at Palm Springs* is also a serious inquiry into the unforeseen extremities of despair that can attend the search for a pure and lasting love."
– *The New York Times*

"Sensitive storytelling."
– *New York Magazine*

OTHER TITLES AVAILABLE FROM SAMUEL FRENCH

DEVIL BOYS FROM BEYOND

Buddy Thomas and Kenneth Elliott
Based on an original script by Buddy Thomas
Original song, Sensitive Girl, music and lyrics by Drew Fornarola

Comedy / 4m, 4f / Unit Set

Flying Saucers! Backstabbing Bitches! Muscle Hunks and Men in Pumps! Wake up and smell the alien invasion in this outrageous comedy by the author of the off-Broadway hit play, Crumple Zone

"***** [FIVE STARS]! Buddy Thomas's deliriously campy sci-fi spoof—one of the most entertaining shows I have ever seen at the Fringe Festival—is naughty, gleeful fun...The show opens a fabulous portal to the past: not just the paranoid world of the 1950s, but the legendary drag romps of Charles Ludlam's Ridiculous Theatrical Company and Charles Busch's Theatre-in-Limbo from the 1960s through the 1980s. Devil Boys from Beyond is a necklace of golden links to that wild theatrical tradition. If there were any justice in this mixed-up world of ours, the whole show would be tractor-beamed *Off Broadway tomorrow.*"
— *Adam Feldman, Time Out New York*

"Cheap in all the right ways, the fast, taw dry and very funny Devil Boys From Beyond is the Fringe Festival at its best."
— *New York Post*

"Devil Boys From Beyond is how a no-budget show should be done... an uproarious homage to C-movies and the golden age of camp!"
—*Backstage*